May Finds Her Way

The Story of an
Iditarod Sled Dog

Story and Illustrations by
Betty Selakovich Casey

The RoadRunner Press
Oklahoma City, Oklahoma

To my children, Connor, Anna, and Mary.
Without you, I wouldn't have had all
those magical years when you said,
"Read me a story!"

Text and illustration copyright © 2013 Betty Selakovich Casey

Published by The RoadRunner Press

Catalog-in-Publication Data is on file at OCLC and SkyRiver and viewable at www.WorldCat.org

ISBN: 978-1-937054-45-8

Printed in November 2013 in the United States of America
by Bang Printing, Brainerd, Minnesota

First Edition November 2013

10 9 8 7 6 5 4 3 2 1

May is happy today. She is going to run a long, long way.

May is a sled dog, but not just any sled dog.

May is an Iditarod sled dog.

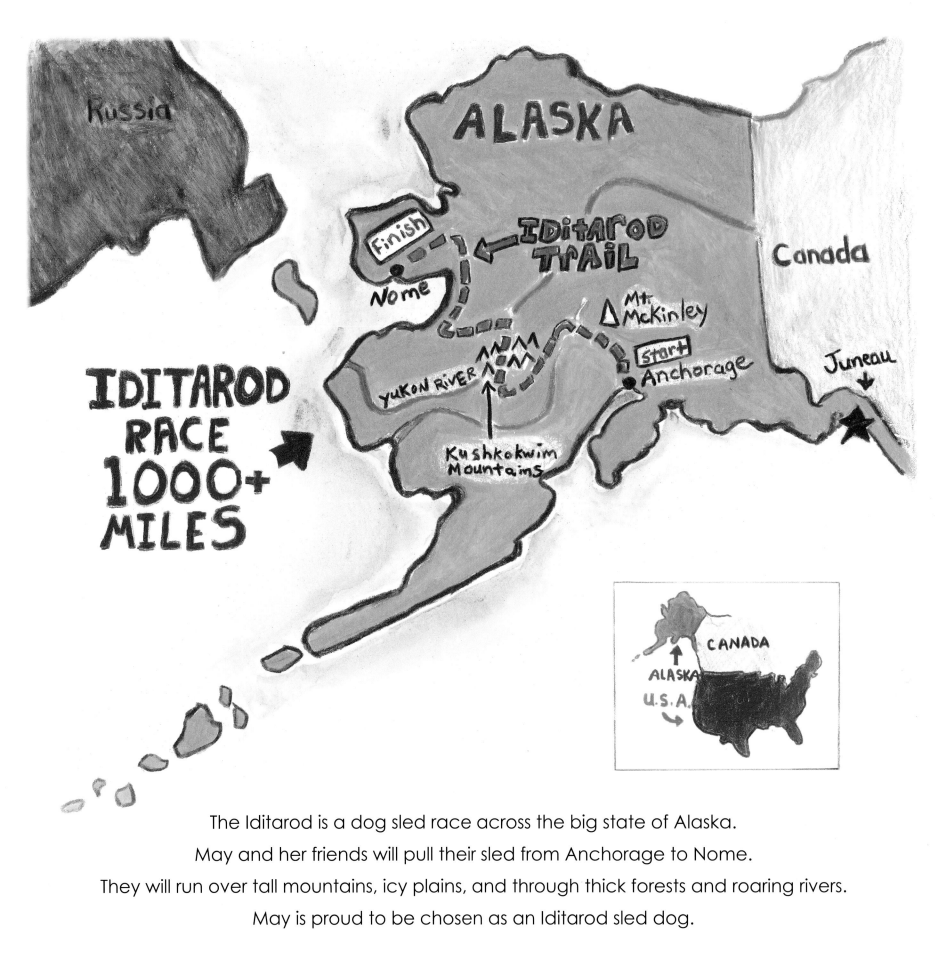

The Iditarod is a dog sled race across the big state of Alaska.

May and her friends will pull their sled from Anchorage to Nome.

They will run over tall mountains, icy plains, and through thick forests and roaring rivers.

May is proud to be chosen as an Iditarod sled dog.

May has friends to help her. May's friend Ajax is the strongest dog on the team.

May's friend Breeze is the fastest dog on the team.

May's friend Juno is the wisest dog. She is the leader.

May wants to be strong, wise, and fast, too, but she is very small.

The sleds line up at the starting line.
Bang! goes the starting gun.
"Mush! Hike! Let's go!" says the sled driver.
May and her friends are on their way!

May is happy to be part of the team.

She loves to help pull the sled over the snow and splash through the streams.

The sun will follow them for many days
as May and her teammates run the Iditarod Trail.

May and her team run all day until the sun disappears behind the mountains.
The dogs and the sled driver rest. May curls up with Breeze to stay warm.
Ukpik, the big Snowy Owl, watches over them.

The March moon tracks across the sky,
and the Northern Lights dance over the Iditarod Trail.

In the morning, the team is ready to go.

"Pull harder, May!" Ajax says as they cross broad streams.

May pulls hard. Her small body strains against the harness.

"Run faster, May," Breeze says as they climb steep mountains.

May stretches her legs to keep up with Breeze.

"Haw! This way!" Juno calls, leading the team around a steep, slippery turn.

May's team runs fast to catch the team ahead of them.

"Pull!" Ajax barks.

"Catch them!" Breeze calls.

"Stay steady!" Juno warns as the sled slips sideways. "We're too close!"

Crash!

It is too late . . .

The two sled teams collide.

The harnesses are tangled.

The dogs bite and snarl.

Soon all the dogs are fighting.

All the dogs except May.

May does not want to fight.

May wants to run.

May slips away

from the fighting sled dogs.

. . . and runs and runs.

May runs away from the growling and the snarling.

May runs away from the shouting of the angry mushers.

May runs a long, long way, deep into the forest.

Ukpik follows May.

May stops.

She listens.

It is very quiet

"Woof?" May barks.

No one answers.

"Woooo! Woooo! Woooo!" May cries.

She listens for Ajax or Breeze

or Juno to answer.

The forest is silent.

May is all alone.

What will May do now? She is afraid. May thinks about Ajax
and Breeze and Juno. How will she find her way home without them?
She isn't strong or fast or wise. And she is lost.

But May loves to run.
She has already run a long, long way.

May will be strong like Ajax.
May will be fast like Breeze.
May will follow the *inuksuk* that marks
the trail like Juno taught her.

And maybe May can find her way
back home along the Iditarod Trail.

May starts running.
She runs through a river.
The freezing water hurts her feet.
May keeps running.

May runs over steep mountains.
She loses her warm boots on the rocky trail.
May keeps running.

May runs and runs until
she is too tired to run any more.

She stops to rest.

Her empty tummy rumbles and growls.
She hears a wolf howl.
He sounds hungry, too.

May is afraid, but she cannot give up.

May knows Ajax and Breeze
and Juno will be
waiting for her at the end of the trail . . .
waiting for her at home.

It is night.

May is lonely, but the forest animals watch over her from the trees.

She curls into a very small ball and sleeps,

dreaming of her warm bed and the salmon she will eat once she is home.

When May wakes, she looks for the Iditarod Trail, but it is gone.

"Wooo! Wooo!" May cries.

"Hoo! Hoo!" Ukpik answers. "I can help you find your way, May. Follow the *inuksuk*!"

May begins to run.

She runs until she sees the *inuksuk*

and a woman with kind eyes

sitting beside a snow machine.

"May! Where have you been?" the woman asks.

"Everyone is looking for you!"

The woman wraps May in a warm blanket.

"You have run a long, long way.

You have been very brave and strong.

You are a smart little dog. I will take you home."

May and the woman arrive in town to a big welcome. "Hooray for May!
Everyone is happy to see May. Children pat her. The newspaperman takes her photo.
Ajax and Breeze and Juno are happy, too.
"We knew you could find your way!" they say.

Happy but tired,

May curls up in her warm, soft bed.

May, the Iditarod sled dog, has found her way.

May goes to sleep dreaming of racing another day.

THE INSPIRATION FOR THIS STORY

There was an actual sled dog, named May, who went missing during the 41st Iditarod Trail Sled Dog Race in 2013. May was lost for seven days and traveled more than 150 miles alone to return home.

A reddish-blonde dog with blue eyes, May had run the Iditarod several times before.

May was from the Northern White Kennels; her musher for 2013 was a sledder from Jamaica.

May is believed to have survived by following the trail back to its start and eating kibble and food scraps left on the course by other dog teams. She was found on a trail that leads to Big Lake by three snow-machiners.

The *inuksuk* (in-ook-shook) is a stone figure built in the image of a person. Originally built by the Inuit, the figures were used to let others know "Someone was here" or "You are on the right path." Including them in the story seemed appropriate.

FACTS ABOUT THE IDITAROD

According to James Kari, professor emeritus of the University of Alaska Native Language Center in Fairbanks, the word *Iditarod* comes from the Deg Hit'an and Holikachuk word, *Xwdedhod*, which means "distant place."

The Iditarod starts outside Anchorage and ends in Nome, Alaska. Its northern trail is used in even years; its southern, in odd years.

More than 1,000 dogs compete on teams each year.

The symbolic length of the race is 1,049 miles (the forty-nine is in honor of Alaska being the 49th state in the union).

The actual race length is about 1,200 miles. It is the longest dog sled race in the world.

The first full length Iditarod race to Nome started March 3, 1973.

As of 2013, Martin Buser held the record for fastest finish — 8 days, 22 hours, 46 minutes, and 2 seconds — set in 2002.

Rick Swenson is the only five-time winner of the Iditarod; he won in 1977, 1979, 1981, 1982, and 1991, but Susan Butcher is a four-time winner (1986, 1987, 1988, 1990) now retired.

Created in the 1920s, the northern and southern sections of the trail are part of the Iditarod National Historical Trail, which once provided the only overland means of travel in the winter. Dog sleds delivered mail and groceries and hauled out gold and furs.

Each year, mushers come from around the world to compete in the Iditarod; those lucky enough to finish cross under an historic Burled Arch from which hangs a "Widow's Lamp." The lamp remains lit so long as there are mushers on the trail competing in the race. For as Alaskans like to say, The race is not over until the last musher has come off the trail.

For more information and lore about the annual Iditarod Trail Sled Dog Race, visit the official website, www.Iditarod.com.